POTATO

A Tale from the Great Depression

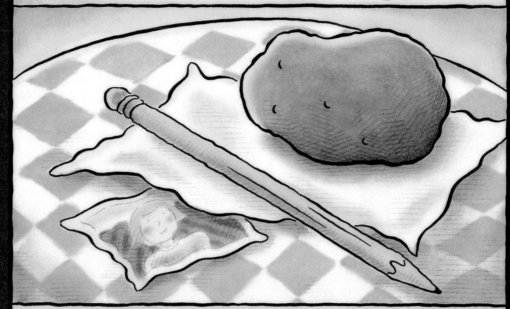

Written by Kate Lied
Illustrated by Lisa Campbell Ernst

NATIONAL GEOGRAPHIC SOCIETY

Washington, D.C. 20036

Distributed by Publishers Group West

Library of Congress Cataloguing-in-Publication Data
Lied, Kate. Potato : a tale from the Great Depression / written by Kate Lied :
illustrated by Lisa Campbell Ernst.   p.   cm.
Summary: During the "Great Depression," a family seeking work
finds employment for two weeks digging potatoes in Idaho.
ISBN 0-7922-3521-5
[1. Depressions—1929—Fiction. 2. Potatoes—Fiction.]
I. Ernst, Lisa Campbell, ill.   II. Title.
PZ7.L6167Po   1997   [E]—dc20   96–11926

This book is dedicated to
my Grandmother and
Grandfather Lied,
who this story is about,
my Aunt Dorothy Wagner,
who passed the story along,
and to Lisa, who believed.
~K.L.

This is a story
about my grandfather
and my grandmother.
It is also a story about
the Great Depression and
how hard things were.

Once upon a time there was a
mother named Agnes and a father named Clarence.

They had a baby girl named Dorothy.

Dorothy and her parents lived in Iowa.
Clarence and Agnes had not been married long.

Clarence lost his job
and the bank took away their house.

Agnes's father had a job in a coal mine
and Clarence joined him.

Then one day the coal mine closed.

There were no other jobs available.

People took jobs wherever they could find them.

Someone they met told them there were jobs in Idaho picking potatoes. Agnes knew someone who had a car they could borrow. So they borrowed money for gas and left Iowa with Dorothy.

For two weeks
they lived in tents.

During the day they picked potatoes.

Dorothy played in the fields, among the potato plants.

The man who owned the farm said that they,
in their own time, at night, could go out in the
picked-over fields and get the leftover potatoes.

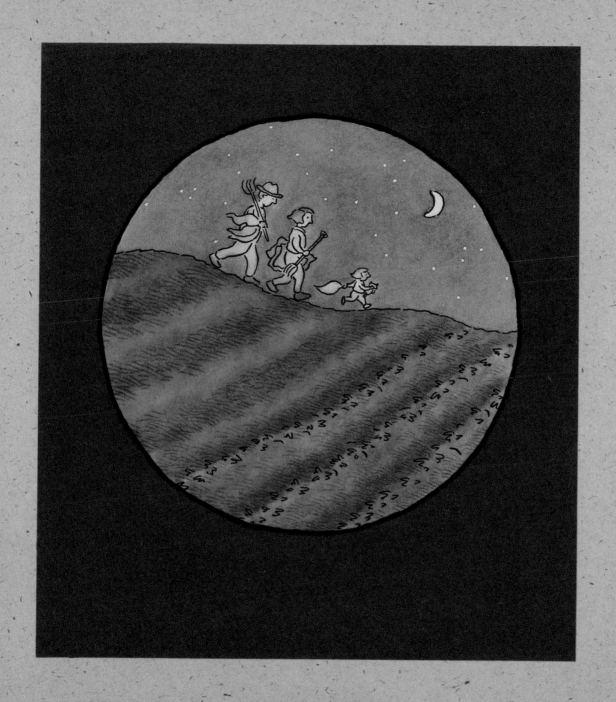

So they bought used burlap sacks
for a penny each. They went out at night and
picked potatoes and put them in the sacks.

The work only lasted two weeks.

They picked potatoes for themselves every night.

At the end of the two weeks they loaded up
Dorothy and the potatoes and headed home. There
were potatoes wherever there was room for potatoes—

on the dashboard, hood, trunk, and running boards.
Dorothy had to sit on the potato sacks. The money
they had earned from working they used for gas.

When they got back home, Clarence and Agnes
traded potatoes for other things: groceries,

clothes, and even a pig. They worked
very hard to live on what little they had.

At last Clarence found a job and the family

moved to Washington, D.C., and then to Hawaii.

Soon Dorothy had two baby brothers,
Bob and Gary. Late at night,

Dorothy told the boys stories of potatoes,
and how they were picked by the light of the moon.

All this
could be
how I have
come to like
potatoes.